Wayward Cat Finds a Home

Dana Trantham

Illustrations by
Brandi Trantham

Wayward Cat Publishing

ISBN: 978-1-938999-14-7
Library of Congress Control Number: 2014948871

Wayward Cat Publishing
Palm Bay, Florida
www.waywardcatpublishing.com

Wayward Cat Finds a Home

Chapter One

The Garage

Wayward Cat was a tiny kitten when he was brought to Mrs. Person's garage in Palm Bay, Florida during a hurricane. He didn't remember being carried by the neck, dangling from his mother's mouth, against the powerful winds. But Mama Cat told him the story many times.

Her kittens were born in a small wood by a ditch when the winds started to blow. She knew she must find shelter for them all, so she set out alone at first, just as it began to rain. The first house she came to was closed up tight. But then she saw the open side door to Mrs. Person's garage, swinging wide, then slamming itself against a concrete block, keeping it from closing. Back and forth the door swung on its hinges. Mama Cat darted inside before the door clanged shut again and knew this was the perfect place to hide her kittens.

So, one by one, she carried them as fast as she could manage and left them on a pile of old towels. With each slam of the door, with every gust of wind, her kittens meowed and were afraid. But Mama Cat cuddled them and told them they were dry and safe and everything would be all right.

Soon after, Mrs. Person rushed into the garage. She kicked the concrete block out of the way of the banging door and closed and locked it. When she turned to go back in the house, she heard something in the corner. There, curled up on the pile of old towels, behind a stack of boxes, she found Mama Cat and her five kittens.

Mrs. Person kept Mama Cat fed and warm even after the storm had passed. She couldn't bring Mama Cat inside, she said, because she had big dogs that would be too curious.

"The garage is not the best place for kittens," she scolded Mama Cat. "But I suppose it had to do in a pinch."

She helped Mama Cat tend her brood, keeping them free of fleas, sweeping up the garage, and providing a sand box for their business. Mama Cat was grateful and once the kittens were up and about, tried to teach them not to play in the sand box.

"That's not for fun," she would tell them.

But it was difficult for them to understand not being able to play in a box full of sand.

Mrs. Person took her time giving the kittens names. Plop was first. Every time Mrs. Person put Plop back on Mama Cat's bed of towels, he lay down and rolled over. "Plop," she would say. "This one plops." Next was Wiggle, because she never let Mrs. Person hold her. "Oh, wiggle, wiggle," she would say. Then Howler and Prissy got their names.

As the weeks passed, Wayward Cat and his brothers and sisters grew and grew and Mrs. Person said she would find homes for them all.

"Why do we need a different home?" Howler cried to Mama Cat.

"You heard her," Prissy said. "A garage is not a proper home."

"That's right, Prissy." Mama Cat said. "One day soon, you will leave me. We will all be safe and fed. That is as it should be."

Mama Cat was full of wisdom and advice and she taught her kittens to clean themselves and to hunt and to purr and to be kind to the people who would help them.

"Purr to those you wish to hear purring back at you," she always said. And, "One day, we will leave this messy place and have real homes."

Wayward Cat thought the garage was a fine place to live and gave no thought to going anywhere else. While his brothers and sisters kept close to Mama Cat, Wayward would rather explore. There was so much to see. Mrs. Person's garage was full of nooks and crannies, spiders and palmetto bugs, lizards and cobwebs. And it was crowded with boxes and bins, rakes and brooms, cans and jars. And strewn about on the floor were screws and nails, tools and pencils, rags and leaves.

"This one is wayward," Mrs. Person said time and time again when Wayward Cat went missing. Each time she found him, she carried him back to Mama Cat and threatened to put him in a box. But Wayward couldn't help himself. He loved his days in the garage and hoped to stay there all his life.

Chapter Two

Wayward Cat's First Adventure

One day, when his brothers and sisters were asleep and the garage was dark, Wayward Cat crawled off the towels and decided to go on a great adventure. I must hike through the jungle to find the stolen treasure belonging to my feline ancestors, he thought. I will sniff it out.

So he sniffed and sniffed and the smells were glorious. He found one particular smell and decided it must be his treasure. He set off in search of it, but came to a great mountain. He jumped and clawed his way up onto small ledges, and then onto rocks and cliffs, higher and higher. And then down the other side of the mountain, he bravely tumbled, landing with a kitten squeak. That was a tall mountain and he was a brave cat to have climbed it, even if he did fall off it rather clumsily.

Now he was in a dark cave with a low ceiling, inching his way forward. The smell of his treasure was very strong here. Something moved up ahead, skittering across his path. Something else was after his treasure! With his powerful cat eyes, he tracked the enemy to its hiding place where he lunged and pounced.

It's a trap! He was caught!

Wayward twisted this way and that, but it was no use. His foe had set out a sticky web to catch him. He would never find the treasure of his feline kin now.

Suddenly the room outside the cave was bathed in light and he heard Mrs. Person counting kittens. One. Two. Three. Four. Where's Wayward Cat? He meowed and tried to get free of the trap he was caught in but it was no use. Finally, Mrs. Person moved the mountain, it was only a small stack of shallow boxes after all, and reached into the cave, which was under a shelf, and pulled him to freedom.

"Oh, Wayward Cat," she said. "What mischief have you gotten yourself into? You're covered in cobwebs."

She took a cloth and wiped Wayward clean.

"Much better."

She cuddled him up against her neck. Pinned onto her dress was a smelly flower with purple petals. He pounced on it and bit it. It tasted almost as good as it smelled. Mrs. Person laughed and held him up to her face again. She rubbed her nose against his and then deposited him back in his mother's nest.

"That was a great adventure," he told his brothers and sisters. He couldn't wait to see what other parts of the garage he could explore.

Every day, Wayward wandered farther and farther from Mama Cat. He pounced lizards and bugs and loved the way they wriggled under his paws.

"Aw, I'm only teasing," he would say and let them go, only to pounce again and giggle.

"Really," he told them. "Only kidding." He set them free once more.

He climbed the shallow boxes and tumbled off them many times, but couldn't jump high enough onto the bigger boxes.

"One day," he told them. "I'll be bigger and climb all the way to the top." But the boxes didn't respond.

Wayward Cat pretended he was a weary traveler, winding in and out of the maze of mountains and hopping over rivers. Sometimes he imagined he was being chased, only to turn and bravely face his predator. Other times he decided he was separated from Mama Cat, lost in a strange land. But most of the time, he sniffed out treasure and found himself covered in dirt, leaves, and cobwebs. The garage was so full of shadows and hidden things, it wasn't so hard to believe in his own imagination.

"You'll never guess what I did today," he would tell his brothers and sisters. And they would sit and purr, and listen to him tell his tales.

When he told them a giant ant chased him all the way to the big metal door, Plop asked, "Did it catch you?" And Howler cried out, "Did it eat you?"

"Almost," Wayward Cat said. "Almost."

Chapter Three

The Cat Adoption

One day, Mrs. Person put Wayward Cat and his four brothers and sisters into a big box that closed up on top. There was a blanket on the bottom to curl up on and holes all around so they could look out and see where Mrs. Person was taking them. But as nice as the box was, they meowed and meowed for Mama Cat. She did not follow.

Mrs. Person brought the kittens to a store harsh with bright lights and echoing with loud voices. They huddled, frightened, in their box until she pulled them out one by one and put them into a cage. All around them were cages with other cats inside them, lounging or sleeping, some hissing, some purring.

"This is the cat adoption," Mrs. Person told them. "You'll find good homes today."

While his brothers and sisters curled up on the blanket, Wayward Cat pounced against the bars and wrestled with feathers and yarn dangling from the top of his cage. He liked his new place. But he had to admit it was too small to capture his imagination for long.

"That one is wayward," Mrs. Person said to the cat rescue volunteers. "Keep a watchful eye on him." They nodded and smiled.

Throughout the day, a volunteer reached into the cage and brought out Wayward Cat's brothers and sisters one by one–Plop and Howler, Wiggle and Prissy–until they were gone and he was alone.

"Don't worry," Miss Lady, one of the volunteers, told him. "All the best ones are saved for last."

But when the long and noisy day ended, Wayward Cat was put back into the box, and Mrs. Person took him home to the garage where he curled up next to Mama Cat and shuddered with sadness. He missed his siblings. Mama Cat purred and cleaned him, her rough tongue soothing his fears. She told him stories and taught him wise things until he fell sound asleep. And after a long nap, he spent all night scurrying around the garage, pouncing and jumping. When he finally returned to Mama Cat, he nudged her awake.

"Where is Howler?" He asked. "Where are Prissy and Wiggle?"

"You know they've found homes," Mama Cat said.

"Yes, but what does that mean? What are homes like?"

Mama Cat pulled Wayward Cat to her and cuddled him. "A home is a place where a cat is loved and pampered. Homes have soft spots in the sunlight where you can nap all day if you like. And homes have enough food so you will never be hungry, and fresh water every day. And a clean box to do your business in. The people there will want to pet you, and hold you, and will let you curl up on their laps and sleep for a while. They're wonderful places and you'll be content when you find one."

"Will you miss me?"

Mama Cat purred. "I will. And you will miss me. But you will soon grow up and be your own cat, as all cats do. You won't be sad. And once in a while, you will smell something particular, and you will remember me, and you will be happy."

"Where will your home be?"

"Don't you worry. I think I will be staying here."

"In the garage?"

Mama Cat chuckled. "No, dear. I will be living with Mrs. Person as an outside cat."

"An outside cat? I want to be one of those, too."

"Inside is better than out."

"Why is that?"

"Dangers and diseases lurk outside. There are predators, and other cats with their territories to defend. It's harder outside."

"Will you be all right?"

"I was always outside. So, yes. I'll be fine. And Mrs. Person will keep me fed and healthy. I will stay here, in her territory. Maybe I'll even make friends with her big dogs and they will protect me. Who knows? Maybe I'll even go inside one day."

"You've never had a home before?"

"No. But I have met many cats on my travels who have, and they told me how wonderful homes can be. And they all wished they had one again. So, remember to always be grateful."

Wayward thought Mama Cat was the wisest cat in the world. He already felt happy and as much as he loved his garage, being pampered and having a soft spot in the sun sounded wonderful. So he played in the garage as often as he could, just in case his new home didn't have dirt and cobwebs and lizards.

"My, my, but you are a mess," Mrs. Person said when she came again with the box. She picked Wayward up and rubbed a cloth all over him. "You've been into the cobwebs again, haven't you?" Into the box he went and he found himself once more at the bright and loud store in a cage with other cats all around.

"This one is wayward," Mrs. Person told the volunteers again. "Keep an eye on him." She tsked a few times and said good-bye. "I'll take good care of Mama Cat," she told him. "Don't you worry. But today, you will be going to your forever home."

Wayward Cat sat in his cage all day long. Only Miss Lady ever took him out and no one asked to take him home. When the cages were being packed away, Miss Lady came to Wayward's cage, reached in, scooped him up and put him in a box. It was just like the one Mrs. Person had, with peep holes and a blanket and a toy mouse to play with. So he was not afraid.

"You're coming home with me," she said.

And so Wayward Cat went home with Miss Lady.

Chapter Four

Miss Lady's House

Miss Lady put Wayward Cat's box in the front seat of her car, right beside her, and she talked and talked all the way home. He tried to listen, but he'd had a long, hard day at the store. So many smells and sights and sounds made him tired; and he had trouble understanding people, anyway.

He could usually figure out what Mrs. Person was saying by the tone of her voice. She was miffed with him when she held him up and said, "Wayward Cat," and had to clean the cobwebs off him. And she was happy with him when she laughed and cuddled him to her neck where she always had a flower pinned.

But Miss Lady was different; she always

sounded happy. And now it was almost as if she were singing. At least he knew he wasn't in any trouble. He purred and purred until he fell asleep. But he woke up as soon as the car stopped.

Wayward Cat watched through the peep holes as Miss Lady carried his box into her house, through a kitchen and a living room, past a fancy room and a den, down a long hallway, and into a small bedroom. Such an enormous place, he thought. She closed the door and put the box down. When she opened the top, Wayward tried to jump out. He landed on Miss Lady's arm.

"Ouch," she cried. "Your claws are small, but they still hurt."

She held him up to her face and said, "Don't do that again, please." And Wayward Cat promised to keep his claws to himself.

Miss Lady showed Wayward around his new room. The bed was next to a window and he knew he could spend days and days curled up on it, watching lizards and butterflies and people and dogs. Outside was a driveway and a street and other houses with windows. Wayward Cat wondered if other cats might sit on their sills sometime and they could watch each other. But he was too excited just now to sit still. He saw a plastic mat on the floor where his food and water bowls were and another mat in the closet for his sand box. He jumped in and skittered about, clawing at the sand and pouncing on it.

"No, no," Miss Lady said, picking him up. "That sand isn't for playing."

And so Wayward Cat promised not to play in the sand. He found a fabric mouse smelling of catnip; and bits of yarn and string lay about for him to wrestle with.

"I have to leave now," Miss Lady said. She pet him, giving him a scratch behind the ears, and left him up on the bed in front of the window. Then she went out and closed the door.

And that's when he heard it–a meow. A deep, scary, awful meow. He sniffed the air and could smell it. Another cat! Wayward's hair stood on end and he arched his back. He loped across the bed sideways and tumbled off it to the floor. It was time for another adventure.

From under the bed, Wayward Cat devised his plan to scout out the enemy. He sniffed and he listened. His enemy lurked behind the great wooden gate of his fort. Scratch, scratch. It was the enemy trying to get in! He must be brave. Slowly, keeping his belly close to the floor of his encampment, Wayward crept out from under his hut and toward the fortress wall. Shadows beneath the gate crossed back and forth. Another guttural meow echoed beyond the halls of his realm and more scratches rattled the gate.

Wayward froze and stared, then crawled some more, lower and lower to the floor, until, finally, he was at the gate. He tried to peer underneath it and sniffed. Wham! A mighty paw struck from under the door and grabbed at him. He shrieked, leapt into the air, arched his back, and skittered backwards into his hut, which was under the bed, of course, where he panted and hissed.

"Get out," the other cat howled from behind the door.

"I..." Wayward stammered. "I can't get out. The door is closed."

"You can't stay here."

Wayward Cat scampered farther under the bed and waited for the big cat to go away. That was enough excitement for one day, he thought. He wondered why Mama Cat didn't say anything about predators inside homes. Maybe they weren't such wonderful places, after all.

Though he wouldn't admit it to Miss Lady, he was too frightened to come out from under the bed for the rest of the day. He didn't mind it so much. There were dust bunnies floating about to be pounced on and dead bugs in the corner to inspect. And so he stayed hidden there until she returned.

Chapter Five

Wayward Cat Meets Squeakers

Wayward Cat spent a long time in his new room with the door closed. Miss Lady visited him several times throughout each day and often checked on him at night. But when she was gone, and the house beyond his room was quiet, the big cat would haunt the outside of his door.

"Go away," Wayward once told him with a hiss.

"You're in *my* house," the old cat said. "You go away."

"Miss Lady brought me here."

"That doesn't mean anything at all. Miss Lady is my person," the old cat said and reached a paw under the door to swat at him. "One day, she'll forget to close this door and then I'll get you. I'll grab you by the scruff of your neck, take you outside, and leave you there."

Wayward shuddered at the thought. He clawed his way up the covers and onto the bed and watched out the window wondering what he would do outside. The outside was too big. He'd be lost. Mama Cat said it was dangerous. He thought for sure Miss Lady meant to keep him. She wouldn't want him to be left alone in the big outside.

"Miss Lady will let me stay," he meowed.

"Not if I can help it."

Maybe the big cat was right. *He* wasn't locked in a room, after all. He must be Miss Lady's cat. And if he told Miss Lady to send Wayward Cat away, why...she just might do it. What should he do?

What would Mama Cat say? He thought and he thought and realized that Mama Cat would tell him you catch more mice with cheese than with claws. He realized he would have to make friends with the old cat, so that he would be allowed to stay with Miss Lady.

One day, after Miss Lady left the house and the old cat patrolled outside his door, occasionally swatting under it, Wayward approached. The big cat stopped his clawing at the air, withdrew his paw and just lay there, sniffing.

"What sort of cat are you?" Wayward asked him.

"I'm bigger than you," he said. "And stronger than you. And I've lived here longer than you. That's what sort I am."

"What's your name?"

"Squeakers."

Wayward purred out a giggle. "That's a funny name. My name is Wayward Cat, because Mrs. Person said I'm wayward. Why are you called Squeakers?"

Squeakers was quiet for a moment, and then he said, "When you get out of that room, I'll show you."

While he thought he might like to explore the big house, Wayward Cat didn't see any reason to ever leave his room. He had everything he could possibly want there and Squeakers couldn't get to him. But he would like to know why a cat would be named Squeakers.

"Do you like string?" Wayward Cat asked.

"Of course I like string."

"Do you like fabric mice with catnip?"

"Of course I do. I'm a cat, aren't I?"

"Do you like to go on adventures?"

Squeakers was quiet for several seconds, then he said, "I don't think so. I like to curl up on my bed near the window. And I like to sleep on Miss Lady's pillow at night. I like to eat my food. But I am almost certain I do not like adventures."

"Well, no cat is perfect, I suppose," said Wayward Cat.

"What's that supposed to mean?"

"It means I like adventures."

Squeakers humphed and stalked away. Later that day, Miss Lady returned home and after a while came to Wayward Cat's door.

"No, no, Squeakers," she said. "Just a moment, please."

When the door opened, Squeakers' loud meow echoed in the hallway and Wayward jumped up, arched and hissing, ready to fight if it came to that. But until it did, he ran to hide under the bed. Miss Lady was able to keep Squeakers out and she closed the door behind her.

"Where are you, kitty?"

Wayward crawled out from under the bed and saw Miss Lady sitting cross-legged on the floor. He loped over and climbed onto her lap, purring.

"Today, you will meet Squeakers," she said.

All he understood was 'Squeakers,' so he continued to romp around, pouncing on bits of yarn and his fabric mouse. Before he knew it, Miss Lady was standing up and opening the door. She scooted out and returned, carrying an enormous, long-haired, colorful monster. Wayward Cat darted under the bed, too afraid even to hiss.

"Oh, come on, Wayward," Miss Lady sang. "It's okay. Squeakers is nice, once you get to know him."

From under the bed, he watched Miss Lady sit cross-legged on the floor, letting Squeakers curl up in her lap. Wayward Cat's eyes were open so wide they ached. He tried to close them up, to look unafraid, but he couldn't. He trembled all over.

"You've smelled each other for days now,"

Miss Lady said. "You're practically brothers."

"Humph," Squeakers said. "I don't have a brother."

"I had two brothers and two sisters when I lived in the garage."

Squeakers hissed. "Go back, then."

"They aren't there anymore. Mrs. Person found them new homes."

"Then she can find you a new home. You can't have mine." Squeakers jumped out of Miss Lady's lap and stalked toward the bed. An eerie whine echoed out of him. "That is *my* fabric mouse," he said. "And that is *my* string. And that is *my* food in your bowl."

Wayward Cat backed up into the darkness under the bed and hissed. Squeakers hissed right back.

"That's enough," Miss Lady said. She scooped Squeakers up and tossed him gently out the door.

From the other side, Squeakers said, "Don't get comfortable. You'll see. If I don't like you, Miss Lady will send you away."

"That went well enough, I suppose." Miss Lady said. She was on her knees, peering under the bed.

Wayward gave her a tiny growl. It was very

hard not to growl when he was scared.

"Tomorrow will be a big day," she said.

When she left him alone and the room gradually went dark with the setting sun, he finally scooted out from under the bed to nibble his kibble.

Chapter Six

The Big Day

The sun woke Wayward Cat early the next morning and he watched the scene outside his window come alive. The large metal door of a garage across the street rolled up and a thin gray-haired man tinkered about inside. A young woman walked around the cul-de-sac pulled by a large black dog on a leash. Two small children ran back and forth in one of the front yards, shouting and laughing, in what looked like rain–but it wasn't raining anywhere else. Mama Cat told Wayward and his brothers and sisters many stories about children. They are people kittens, she said. But as he watched the boy and girl play, he didn't see them stalk and pounce on anything–not even once. He decided they weren't like kittens, after all.

Wayward also saw the tiny things outside his

window. A beetle made its way, ungainly, across the driveway. Bits of acorn fell from the oak tree in the yard, as a squirrel up high on a branch nibbled away at it. He jumped up and swatted at a lizard on the glass and rolled over on the bed with giggles when it leapt in fear.

"Silly lizard."

The trees were full of birds and he could hear their songs and chirping even through the window. The squirrel dropped its acorn when it saw him and shrieked.

"Cat!" It said. "Cat, cat, cat."

"Silly squirrel," Wayward said. "I can't get you through the glass."

When the door opened, he turned. Miss Lady came into the room and picked up his food and water bowls to clean and fill them as usual. But she forgot to close the door behind her when she left.

"Miss Lady," he called after her. "The door."

And just as Wayward Cat feared, Squeakers appeared in the hallway and sat, glaring at him. Miss Lady returned, nearly tripping over the big cat.

"Today is the day," Miss Lady said. "You can explore the whole house."

She picked Wayward up off the bed and set him on the floor. Then she went to Squeakers and grunted as she lifted him.

"You need to go on a diet," she said. She put Squeakers in the room across the hall and closed the door. "You have the house to yourself for a while. And then we'll let Squeakers join you."

Wayward Cat thought he understood and walked to the open doorway. He followed Miss Lady warily out of the room and down a long hallway into the main part of the house. He remembered these rooms. He saw them from the peep holes in his box when Miss Lady brought him home. At the time, he'd only caught tiny bits of the smells. Now he breathed them all in, memorizing them.

Wayward Cat got right down to exploring. In the first room, everything smelled clean and a little bit like flowers. He tried to remember where he'd smelled them before. Oh, yes. It was Mrs. Person and the flower she had pinned on her dress. He searched and searched for the flower, but never found it. A couch, striped in many colors, sat against one wall; it smelled like it belonged to Squeakers.

In front of the couch was a glass table that he

could get under and look up at the bottoms of the things sitting on top of it. He pounced upward at them, just to see what would happen. Nothing did. He jumped up on top and sniffed at the earthy aroma of a waxy candle and then pawed at it. A frozen statue of a cat had an old smell to it and next to it he found a withered, dried up tree branch.

Something shiny caught his eye.

"What's that?"

It was at the other end of the table. A bowl as big as he was. Filled with...rocks! Smooth, colorful rocks. He swished his paw in the bowl and tried to scoop one out. It fell back. Plop! So he stepped into the bowl, instead, and skittered about with the rocks.

Then he saw a window with a low, wide sill that he thought he could reach. He hopped out of the rock bowl, off the table and across the room, where he managed to leap up onto the sill. Outside he could see an orchid tree and more oak trees and shrubs covered in bugs and butterflies.

In the next room, bookcases lined one wall. They sat much too low to crawl under, but he was able to climb behind the books on the bottom shelf and hide there. He stayed hidden for a while, scampering about with the dust bunnies, imagining he was in his dark cave back in the garage. He knew he could have excellent adventures behind the books. When he scuttled out, he was covered in dust. He sneezed–kerchoo!–and wished Mrs. Person was there to wipe him clean.

By a corner window, sat a big, puffy chair. He hopped onto it, clawed his way upward to the top, and looked out at the same front yard and driveway he could see from his room. There was that squirrel again.

"Silly squirrel."

And down below, behind the puffy chair, he saw a small table with a big soft bed on it. That must be Squeakers' bed by the window, he thought. I'd better stay out of it.

Wayward found still another room with another big sofa in it and more shelves filled with things he could knock over. And the kitchen held all sorts of strange smells, but when he searched everywhere for the delicious things he knew must be there, he couldn't find anything.

After he explored all the rooms in that part of the house, he peered back down the hallway. At that end of the house, there was more to discover, but he'd have to pass by the door where Squeakers was locked away. He decided against it. Instead, he found the big, puffy chair at the corner window again, climbed onto it, and licked himself clean all over. Finally, he curled himself up for a nap.

"This was a nice day," he said with a purr.

He was all set to sleep when he heard a door in the hallway creak open.

Chapter Seven

How Squeakers Got His Name

Wayward smelled Squeakers before the big cat appeared at the end of the hallway. He jumped up and fell off the chair to the floor–onto his feet, of course. There he was, sitting a few feet away from him, glaring at him with a smirk.

"Now, I'll be right here," Miss Lady said. "You two behave yourselves." She disappeared around the corner into the kitchen.

Wayward Cat looked at Squeakers and they both sat for a long time. Finally, he put on a friendly purr and walked cautiously over to him. He sat and pawed at the carpet a few times, nervous.

"Hi, Squeakers," he said. "You want to go on

an adventure with me?"

"No."

"I found a lot of places to hide and pounce and pretend."

"No."

"I found a bowl of rocks in the fancy sitting room. We could knock it off the table. I tried, but I need help."

"No."

"There's a dusty place behind the books."

"No."

Wayward Cat let out a purry sigh. "Well. You said when I got out of my room, you'd tell me how you got your name. You want to do that?"

"I said I'd *show* you."

"Okay. Show me."

Suddenly, Wayward was flat on the ground underneath the large, old cat. He squeaked.

Squeakers sat harder. He squeaked again and

Miss Lady came into the room.

"Squeakers! Get off him."

But Squeakers didn't move and Wayward Cat squeaked again. It was the darnedest thing. He couldn't seem to help himself. It was as if he were a noisy toy and all Squeakers had to do was smash him and out blurted the squeak.

Miss Lady lifted Squeakers off and scolded him kindly before putting him back down. "We don't squeak others, remember? Now behave." Then she disappeared again into the kitchen.

"And that's how I got my name."

"I don't think I've ever been squeaked before," Wayward Cat said.

Squeakers sighed. "It's one of my many talents." Then he hissed and pounced, and sat on Wayward again.

Wayward Cat let out another squeak.

"Squeakers!" Miss Lady called from the kitchen. "I'm warning you."

Squeak!

"Squeakers, do I have to come in there again? Because if I do..."

Squeak!

Squeak.

Miss Lady stomped in and pulled the big cat

off him. "I will put you in your room if you do that again."

Miss Lady was very angry and Wayward Cat realized she wouldn't always sound like she was singing. She scolded Squeakers some more, then put him back down and left.

Wayward wished Miss Lady wouldn't keep leaving.

"You made Miss Lady mad," he said. "You probably shouldn't do that anymore."

Squeakers shrugged and licked a paw. "Miss Lady is never really angry."

"Hasn't she put you in your room before?"

"Sure. When I bring in frogs and lizards. Or if I swat one of the kids who comes over. Or if I get into a fight with a cat outside a window."

"You didn't mind being put in your room?"

"It calms me down. It's for my own good."

"Does that mean you're going to squeak me some more?"

"I figure I can squeak you twice before getting put on time out," Squeakers said. "I think twice a day will be enough to let Miss Lady know that you don't belong here."

Chapter Eight

Days of Being Squeaked

Miss Lady let Wayward Cat and Squeakers play together more and more often. Wayward would pounce on the fabric mice, leap at the strings dangling from little fishing poles attached to the walls, romp across the tiled floors and claw furiously at the carpets. And Squeakers would sit and watch him, waiting to strike.

Miss Lady let Squeakers squeak Wayward longer and longer before she stopped him, until he realized she wanted to see what he would do. She was waiting to see if Wayward would get himself out from under the big cat by himself. But he was so heavy. And Wayward Cat was so small. Still, he set out to try it each time. Squeakers would pounce and Wayward would squeak. Then he would wriggle this way and wriggle that way and squeak again.

"It's no use," Squeakers said.

"Oh, yeah. Well one day, you'll see."

"One day you'll be gone."

This always made Wayward Cat very sad.

Over time, Wayward realized that Squeakers wasn't going to do anything more than hiss at him and sit on him. Miss Lady must have realized it, too, because she left them alone for longer and longer periods of time, until Wayward Cat's door was always open. And one day, Miss Lady picked up his food and water bowls and never brought them back. She carried him into the room across the hall, past a large bed and dressers, and into a bathroom.

"There you are," she said as she put him down in front of his food bowl. "You and Squeakers can eat together from now on."

This was not a good idea and Wayward Cat knew it. Before Miss Lady could leave the room, Squeakers was on top of him and he was being squeaked.

"Squeakers," she shouted and the big cat hopped off him and went to his bowl.

"I'm eating with you now," Wayward said. "That must mean I get to stay."

"Don't count on it. You think you're the first

kitten Miss Lady has brought home for a short visit? They come and go like mice around here. No. One day you'll be gone and I'll have my house to myself again. And none too soon."

"But aren't you lonely? Who do you have adventures with?"

"I told you, I don't like adventures. I can sit by windows and curl up on chairs all by myself, thank you very much."

"Sounds boring to me."

Squeakers glared at Wayward Cat for a few seconds and then casually walked over and sat on him until he squeaked.

"Squeakers!" Miss Lady yelled from another room.

The big cat got off him again and went back to eating. "I can squeak you more often if I just get off when I'm told," he said. "Are you going to eat that?"

Wayward nibbled on a bit more food from his bowl, but he was too sad to finish. "I suppose I've eaten all I can this morning."

"I'll help you," Squeakers said and took a turn at Wayward Cat's bowl.

"It's no wonder you're such a fat cat."

Squeakers looked up from eating, grinned,

and pounced again, making Wayward squeak and burp. He jumped off and went back to eating before Miss Lady could scold him.

And so Squeakers was up to four squeaking sessions a day when Miss Lady was home.

One day, when Miss Lady was away at that place she spent most of her time, Wayward Cat left his room and went in for breakfast. Squeakers glared at him.

"Will you be squeaking me this morning?" Wayward asked. "I'd prefer to be squeaked before breakfast, if you don't mind."

"Why bother when Miss Lady isn't here?"

"I thought you liked squeaking me."

"I have more important things to do than smash you into the floor."

He was glad of that. "I'm going to have an adventure today. Would you like to join me?"

"No."

Wayward Cat finished his breakfast and curled up on the big, puffy chair in the den for his morning nap. When he woke, he sniffed the air.

"I must find the secret to not being squeaked," he said. "The secret resides with the wise old cat on top of the mountain."

"Who are you talking to?" Squeakers called to

him from the kitchen, where he was curled up on a chair at the table.

"I'm having an adventure," Wayward told him.

"Well, do it quietly, please. I'm napping."

Wayward Cat stretched and hopped off the chair. "It will be a long, hard trek," he whispered. "But I can do it."

Wayward sidled along the walls of his den, wary of the dangers of the world outside. He darted across the opening of his large cave and found himself in the jungles of the living room where the strange tall creatures did their living. There, before him, sat Mount Sofa. He climbed onto the seat, his strong claws lifting his body up and up. Then he climbed the back of it, to the top, and from his perch, surveyed the jungle floor beneath him.

"I alone will possess the secret to not being squeaked," he said.

"Oh, be quiet," Squeakers mumbled.

Wayward Cat faced the cliff behind Mount Sofa and knew he must scale it to the top of the world. He grabbed at it with his claws, caught hold, and climbed and climbed. Up to the very top and then...

"Help," he howled. "Help me."

Wayward turned to look down at Squeakers in the doorway looking up at him.

"How did you get up there? Miss Lady doesn't allow cats to claw the curtains."

"I climbed," he cried.

"It's a good thing you're still small. If you pulled the curtains off the wall, Miss Lady might really get mad for once."

"How do I get down?"

"I'm sure I don't know; I'd never misbehave in such a way," Squeakers said with a shrug.

"You never climbed the curtains?"

He chuckled. "Don't be absurd."

Wayward Cat howled some more.

"It won't do you any good yelling. Miss Lady isn't home."

"What do I do?"

"You'll have to let go."

"Let go?" Wayward couldn't possibly let go. Could he? He was up so high. Everything down below was so far away. He could see the top of the sofa where he'd first caught hold of the curtains. If he dropped, perhaps he would land there.

"Well, go on then." Squeakers said.

"Okay, I'm going to let go."

Wayward Cat howled once more in protest at the very idea, then closed his eyes and pulled his claws back in. He tumbled from the curtain and landed on the top of the sofa. Plop! Then bounced off and fell behind it to the floor.

Squeakers laughed so hard he sneezed and then poked his head behind the sofa. "Did you land on your feet?" He asked. "All good cats land on their feet."

"Yes," Wayward murmured. "I did."

"And are you hurt?"

Wayward Cat thought a moment about each part of him. "My paw is a bit sore." Then he smiled. "What a great adventure that was!"

Chapter Nine

Miss Lady's Garage

"I told you that you don't belong here," Squeakers said as Wayward Cat shimmied out from behind the couch. "We don't climb the curtains here."

"Well, if not here, where *do* I belong?"

"You said you lived in a garage before. I think that's where you're supposed to be."

"But Mrs. Person took me out of the garage."

"It doesn't matter. You can take the cat out of the garage, but you can't take the garage out of the cat."

"What does that mean?"

"It means you belong in a garage."

"Does Miss Lady have a garage?"

"Of course she does. I'll show you."

Squeakers stalked off and Wayward Cat followed him, out of the living room, through the kitchen, and into a small, dark laundry room, to a big white door.

"There it is," Squeakers said.

"That's a door."

"I know what it is. Behind it is another door you can see through, and smell through. You wouldn't believe all the wonderful smells floating about in the garage."

"Why is the door closed?"

"Miss Lady only opens the door when she wants air in the house. Then I get to sit here and smell all of the smells of the garage and the outside."

"The outside?" Wayward loved looking at the outside from the window in his room. While he could smell some of the stronger odors through the glass, to be able to smell everything outside would be wonderful.

"That's right. A very loud, very large door rolls right up into the roof and when it's open, I can see and smell the outside. And when this door is open, the back door is open, too. The one in the living room where you fell behind the couch."

"Don't remind me," Wayward Cat said, licking his sore paw.

"When the back door is open, I can walk right into the outside."

"What? You go outside?"

"Well, sort of. It's an outside room. I can sit on a chair and look out through a screen and watch birds and squirrels."

"Oh, that sounds like such an adventure! When can we do it?"

"We? Don't be silly. You don't belong here, remember? That's *my* outside room. You need to go into the garage."

"What if I don't want to?"

Squeakers shrugged. "If there's one thing I've learned, it's that it doesn't matter all that much what we want. If it's time to go to the vet, for instance, Miss Lady will find some way to get me into the carrying box. She's very sneaky. And if it's time to come in from the outside room, she makes me do it. An inside cat only has so much freedom."

"But aren't you grateful for being able to live here with Miss Lady?"

"Of course. A good cat is always grateful. And I'll be even more grateful when Miss Lady puts you out in the garage where you belong."

"Is that where she put the other cats?"

"Oh, no. She took them very far away. I hope she takes you far away, too. And leaves you there. But the garage is better than nothing."

Suddenly a roar erupted on the other side of the white door and Wayward Cat scrambled out of the laundry room, slipping and sliding on the tiled floor, and back into the kitchen.

"What is it?"

"It's the big rolling door I told you about. Miss Lady is home."

Sure enough, after a loud bang and a rattling sound, the white door opened and Miss Lady stepped in. For a moment, Wayward Cat caught a whiff of grease and dirt and trash and remembered his old garage home at Mrs. Person's house. It made him think of Mama Cat and his brothers and sisters. Then the white door closed and Miss Lady came into the kitchen and reached down to pet Squeakers as he wriggled about at her feet.

When Miss Lady stepped away from Squeakers and toward him, Wayward Cat backed himself up against the kitchen cabinets.

"What's the matter, Wayward?" Miss Lady said.

She scooped him up into her arms and he wiggled about trying to get free. He did not want to go into the garage.

"Poor kitty," she said. She rubbed behind his ears and kissed him on the head before setting him back down.

"She didn't put me out," he told Squeakers, breathless and trembling.

"Humph," the old cat said. "Soon enough, I'm sure."

Wayward Cat shivered and trotted back to his room and under the bed. What if Squeakers was right? What if Miss Lady was going to put him in the garage? Miss Lady already had Squeakers, after all. What would she need another cat for? Especially one that climbed the curtains?

The next morning, something was different.

Chapter Ten

The Big Outside

When Wayward Cat woke up, the house was cooler. The air smelled different. Bits of flowers and grass and dogs and lizards mingled in the aromas all around him. He crawled out from under his bed and made his way into the hall, sniffing. His stomach growled.

"I heard that," Squeakers said from the bathroom inside the big room.

Wayward found him by the food bowls.

"Have you eaten my food yet?" Wayward Cat asked.

"See for yourself."

Luckily, Wayward's food was still in the bowl. He'd never grow big and strong with Squeakers eating up all his leftovers, but he just couldn't eat as much in one sitting as the big cat could. And it was even harder to concentrate on eating when adventure called from every piece of furniture in the house.

After a few bites, he asked Squeakers, "What's the smell?"

"It's an outside day."

"We're going outside?"

"Well, I am. Into the outside room I told you about; it's called the porch."

"Porch? That's a funny name."

"The big doors are open and only those screen doors and windows stand between me and the outside."

Wayward Cat was excited, but also frightened. What if Miss Lady put him out and didn't let him back in?

As if reading his mind, Squeakers said, "Maybe today is the day you finally go away and don't come back."

Wayward let out a sorrowful meow and sat back from his bowl. He couldn't eat the rest. He was too upset.

"Are you going to finish that?" Squeakers said.

"You go ahead."

"Well, what are you waiting for then? Go on outside. If you see an open door, don't hesitate to use it."

He thought about it and decided he would wait for Squeakers. When the big cat finally finished all the food and they both took their turns in the sand boxes and had some water, he followed him out of the room and down the hallway. As soon as they left the hall, the smells of the outside world hit Wayward like a symphony. A slight, damp breeze sent wonderful chills across his back.

"The windows out here are open, too." Squeakers said.

They kept on, through the den with the puffy chair and bookcases and into the living room where Wayward had his adventure climbing the curtains. And there he saw a set of double doors wide open, just like Squeakers said. An outside room!

Wayward paused at the opening and sniffed the marvelous outdoor odors before him. Then he stepped gingerly onto the concrete floor; it chilled his paws. Chairs sat around a big table on one side of the room and on the other, there was a long bench where he imagined Squeakers liked to curl up and nap. The walls of the outside room rose only to the height of Squeakers when he stood on his hind legs. Wayward knew this because the first thing the big cat did was walk to the outer wall and stand up, putting his front paws on a little ledge.

"Are you going to jump out?" Wayward asked him.

"Don't be silly. It's covered in screen."

"What is screen?"

"It's a wall you can see through," Squeakers said.

"What do you see?" Wayward wished he was a grownup cat.

"Humph," Squeakers said. "Go look out one of the doors and leave me alone."

Wayward Cat saw the two screen doors and loped over to the closest one to look out into the back yard. Just outside the screen was a patch of ferns surrounding flowering plants and a tall, twisted orchid tree. In front of it, a tiny wooden house hung from a hook on a pole. The house was filled with birdseed and a fat squirrel sat atop it. When he saw the two cats peering at him, he darted away and started shrieking.

"Where did he go?" Wayward asked.

"He's over here," Squeakers said. "In the oak tree. I've got my eye on him."

"I could have such a great adventure out here."

"Oh, you and your silly adventures. Stalk something. Be a real cat."

"I'm on a great squirrel hunting expedition. I'm the greatest squirrel hunter who ever lived!"

"Humph," Squeakers said.

Wayward Cat stalked each piece of furniture on the porch, pounced at the legs, clawed his way up onto the seats, and attacked a plate of rocks on the table.

"Miss Lady likes rocks," he said.

"Don't bother me," Squeakers said. "Can't you see I'm stalking the squirrel."

"You're just standing there watching it."

"That's what stalking is."

Wayward knew better than that. Mama Cat

had taught him. Stalking meant skittering sideways, sneaking up, hunching down, and pouncing. He hopped from the table, back to a chair, and then hung from the soft part for a second before letting himself drop down to the cold concrete floor.

He snuck along one wall to the other door and was surprised to find it ajar.

Chapter Eleven

Wayward Cat is Lost

Wayward Cat put his nose in the crack between the door and the porch wall and sniffed. The air outside was glorious. He pushed against the door. He must stalk the great squirrel and show Miss Lady what a good cat he really is, he thought. He pushed again. He put his whole body against the door and walked it out until it was wide open. Then he looked up and saw a street just as a car raced past the house. He squeaked! He jumped! And the door slammed shut behind him.

He was outside!

"Um. Squeakers?"

Squeakers didn't answer him. A butterfly dipped from above and flitted in front of his face. He reached up a paw and swatted at it but it flew away, along the wall of the porch. Wayward

Cat followed.

"I must stalk the butterfly, pounce on it, and bring it back to Miss Lady," he said. "When Miss Lady sees that I can bring her gifts, she'll keep me forever."

He followed the fluttering yellow wings around to the back of the porch where he could see Squeakers' head peeking out above the wall behind the screen, his ears flat and his eyes wide. He was still watching the shrieking squirrel up in the oak. The butterfly led Wayward on until he found himself in the patch of ferns he'd seen earlier.

"I must trudge through the fern jungle and find a giant snake to take back to Miss Lady," he said as he dove into the tall green fronds.

He danced and jumped and pounced and wriggled and played until he emerged on the other side with dirty paws and bits of fern stuck in his fur. He bounced about in the thick grass; it was cool and damp on his paws. When he saw a lizard perched on a slim blade, he squatted down on his belly and wiggled his bottom. His ears lay flat and he almost growled.

"I will pounce you!"

Wayward Cat leapt out of the grass and landed on top of the lizard. He hopped off it and batted it with his paw as it ran from him.

"Stop," he said. "Let's play."

But the lizard continued hopping and running across the lawn until it made its way up a tree covered with rough, flaky ovals of bark. The butterfly dipped in front of him again and Wayward Cat was off, chasing him, jumping and twisting in the air after him, until finally, he plopped down in the cool, shaded grass, exhausted.

When he finally caught his breath, Wayward looked about him. Where was the orchid tree and the patch of ferns? Where was the porch? Houses stood all around. One behind him. One in front. One to this side and one to that. The cul-de-sac, with a patch of weeds in the middle, was familiar. He was sure he'd seen it from his window. And the houses, too. But which one was Miss Lady's house? Where was his home?

"Oh, no," he cried. "I've put myself outside."

Wayward Cat began to howl. He whined and meowed and howled some more. But he felt so tiny in the big outside; his little voice didn't seem to travel at all. He walked this way and that, searching for the porch. The butterfly was back, dipping down toward him and up into the air. But Wayward didn't dare follow him any more. He cried and cried.

"Oh, for pity's sake," Squeakers said from far away. "What is it, now?"

"I'm lost!" Wayward meowed. "Where are you?"

"I'm in the outside room, of course. Where are you?"

"I told you. I'm lost. Help!"

"What am I supposed to do?"

Wayward Cat howled and howled until finally, he heard Squeakers howling with him. The big cat's meows echoed throughout the neighborhood like a siren. Somewhere far away a dog barked.

"Stop," Wayward cried. "You're calling the dogs!"

But Squeakers couldn't hear him. The old cat meowed and meowed. Wayward crouched low in the grass, prepared to run if any dog should come loping toward him. Suddenly, the howling stopped. Wayward listened as hard as he could. Had Squeakers gone back inside? Then he heard another sound. It was Miss Lady.

"What is it?" She was saying. "What's wrong?"

Squeakers meowed again and again, until one of the screen doors creaked open and banged closed and Miss Lady walked from behind the house in front of him.

"Wayward!" She cried.

Miss Lady came to him, scooped him up into her arms and cuddled him. Was he ever glad to see her! He purred and curled up into a ball and let her carry him back to the porch.

"How did you get outside?" She said. "If it hadn't been for Squeakers' howling, I might have lost you forever."

"Well, that's just great," Squeakers said when Miss Lady put Wayward Cat down in front of him. "I should have kept my big mouth shut."

Shaking and crying from his ordeal, Wayward could only purr and offer a head butt to

Squeakers' legs.

Squeakers said, "Humph," and walked away.

"What an amazing adventure." But Wayward Cat was still trembling.

Chapter Twelve

A Scary Place

The next morning, after breakfast and two squeakings, Wayward Cat walked out into the den prepared to take his morning nap on the puffy chair by the front window. Before he could settle down, Miss Lady came over, picked him up, carried him into the kitchen, and put him into a thick plastic box. She closed a gate in the front of it and he was trapped inside. This was not the same box he'd been in before.

"Squeakers," Wayward called. "Squeakers, what's happening? Am I going away now?"

The large cat ambled into the kitchen, got a quick scratch on the head from Miss Lady then plopped down in front of the box.

"It looks like it's time for you to leave," Squeakers said. "It's been nice meeting you. Enjoy your new home."

"But I don't want a new home. I like this one."

"Of course you do. My home is wonderful."

"Oh, no," Wayward Cat cried.

"Don't worry about it. Miss Lady would never leave you at a bad place."

"Oh, no," he said again.

Miss Lady returned and lifted his box into the air.

"Good-bye, Squeakers. I'll miss you."

"Humph," the old cat said.

Wayward Cat curled up in the back of the box during the short car ride while Miss Lady said soothing things that didn't soothe him at all. He didn't pounce. He didn't peek out the holes in the box. He sat and waited and hoped his new home would be a nice one. The car stopped and Miss Lady got out and carried his box to a building. Before they entered, Wayward Cat smelled the noisy outside. The air was filled with pungent, acrid odors. A car horn sounded. This couldn't be a very nice place, he thought. He smelled no flowers at all.

Once inside, the noises changed. Dogs. Lots of dogs. They were barking, and whining, and their claws pricked at the tiled floor as they danced about. Their sounds bounced off the walls. And they smelled like the laundry room at Miss Lady's house.

"Oh, dear." Wayward Cat sat up and peered through the holes as Miss Lady set the box down at her feet. Dogs everywhere! He arched his back and hissed. A clumsy Labrador bounded over and stuck his face against the holes, his tongue shaking drool. He licked the box.

Wayward Cat panicked. He dashed this way and that and finally up against the gate. It opened! He darted out.

The dog barked. More dogs wailed. Miss Lady yelped and Wayward ran and ran. He skidded into a wall. More humans yelled. Hands grabbed at him. The Labrador came at him but was choked back by a leash. He ran again, into a hallway. Cats howled. Dogs whined. A machine hummed. He ran and ran until he was trapped in another room and crawled between boxes, his face hiding in the dark, panting.

After a few minutes, Wayward caught his breath and began to cry.

"What's wrong with you?" A cat said.

Wayward looked up, but saw nothing but stacks of boxes above him. He'd wedged himself between them.

"I said," the cat purred. "What's wrong with you?"

Wayward wriggled his bottom and managed to back out from between the boxes only to find they were large cages with gates for doors, very much like his new box, but bigger. Inside one sat a skinny black cat with a white patch of fur on his nose.

"I'm frightened," Wayward Cat said.

"That much is obvious."

"Is this my new home? It's awful."

"I'll grant you that," the cat said. "My name is Mittens. And you are?"

"I'm Wayward Cat."

"Yes. Obviously."

"Do we all live in cages here?"

"We don't *live* here." Mittens looked around at the other cages and Wayward let his gaze follow.

The room was filled with large boxes and many had other cats inside them, watching him.

"You don't?"

"We stay here while our people have to be away. They always come back for us."

Wayward felt a touch of relief, but wasn't certain. "But, Miss Lady left Squeakers at home. She must not be going anywhere. Maybe I have to live here."

"He's from the bad place," one of the other cats said.

"The bad place?" Wayward said.

"The place where they poke you with a pin and force you to drink medicine."

"It's a terrible, terrible place," Mittens agreed.

"I don't want to live there, either." Wayward said.

"You don't *live* there. You get vaccinated there."

Wayward didn't understand. Before he could ask more questions, a person came into the room and picked him up. "There you are," she said.

"Good luck, Wayward," Mittens said. "And be brave."

That wasn't a very good adventure, Wayward thought.

Chapter Thirteen

The Womp Room

It was just as the other cat said. Wayward was poked with a pin a few times and prodded and weighed. But when the ordeal was over, Miss Lady let him back in his box and took him home. She set the box in the kitchen and opened the gate.

Squeakers walked toward him. "You're back." When he got to the gate he stopped, stepped back, and hissed. "You smell like the vet."

"Now Squeakers," Miss Lady said. "Be nice. Wayward has had a hard day."

When Wayward Cat stepped out of his box, Squeakers hissed again and swatted him with a big paw. Miss Lady tried to pick him up, but he hissed and swatted her as well.

"What's wrong?" Wayward asked.

"The vet," he said. "I don't like the vet."

Miss Lady scolded Squeakers and he ran back into his bedroom. Wayward was worried about the old cat, but he was also drowsy and achy. He went to the puffy chair in the den, but was too tired to climb onto it. Miss Lady lifted him gently and set him down on it; he curled up and went to sleep.

When he woke, Wayward saw Squeakers sitting on the floor staring at him.

"I think I get to stay," he told him sleepily. "Miss Lady didn't leave me anywhere."

"Don't count on it," Squeakers said. "She only took you to the vet to make sure you are well enough to be given to another person."

"How do you know?"

"It's happened before. I'm telling you. This is *my* home. You're not staying."

The big cat turned and stalked away.

Wayward's body was sore as he plopped to the floor from his puffy chair. He made his way down the hall and into the big bathroom to his bowl where he nibbled a few kibbles and had some water. Then he went across the hall to his room and crawled under the bed.

"Squeakers said Miss Lady wouldn't send me away to a bad place. But the vet was terrible." He curled himself up and cried himself to sleep.

Wayward slept all through the night and when he woke the next morning, it was to loud bumps and scraping noises against one of the walls of his room. He crept warily out from under the bed and WOMP! He jumped.

"Squeakers," he called. But the big cat didn't answer.

At the door, Wayward peered down the hall.

WOMP! SHIMMY! SCRAPE!

The noise was coming from the back end of the house, from the room next to his that always had its door closed. Wayward hadn't been able to explore in there at all. But now he saw a shadow moving about in the hall and the door stood open. A womp monster could lurch into the hallway at any moment.

WOMP! Wayward leapt into the air and backed up into his room. Fearing the scraping and rustling, he crept to the door again.

"Squeakers?" He said.

"I'm down here," Squeakers hissed.

Wayward turned and saw Squeakers peering out from the living room at the other end of the house. The old cat was bobbing his head up and down, as if trying to see what might emerge from the back bedroom.

"What's the noise?"

WOMP! Squeakers disappeared and Wayward jumped. When Squeakers' face appeared around the corner again his eyes were wide with alarm.

"Miss Lady is moving things," he said.

Oh, well, Wayward thought. If it's just Miss Lady. He walked down the hall to the open door, dared to look into the room and saw Miss Lady standing in the center surrounded by enormous brown boxes. Wayward watched as she dug through one, shook her head, picked it up and tossed it to another pile. WOMP!

"It has to be here somewhere. I just know it is," Miss Lady cried.

Wayward backed up a few paces. Miss Lady was upset, just like when she had to yell at Squeakers for squeaking him. Now she was upset with the boxes. He watched as she moved them from one place to another, ran a blade across the tops of them, dug into them, tossing out packing paper, then closing them up, shoving them aside or piling them up again.

Finally, she stopped and turned to look at Wayward in the doorway. He backed up a bit, worried she would scold him, but she laughed.

"This is quite a pickle, isn't it, Wayward?" She said. "I suppose I'm just going to have to unpack everything and put it in its place. Then we'll find the pencil sharpener. Won't we?"

Wayward had no idea what Miss Lady was talking about. Squeakers had snuck up the hallway and sat beside him.

"I suppose you think you're very brave," he said.

"It was only Miss Lady. What are all the boxes?"

"We brought them from our small place, where we lived before."

"How long have you lived here?"

"A long time now. I guess Miss Lady didn't empty them all. Just wait until she does. The boxes are the best toys ever. Even I enjoy them. I imagine you'd have great adventures with them."

Wayward beamed at the old cat, hardly believing he'd heard him correctly.

"You mean, I can stay? And play in the boxes?"

Squeakers stood tall and lifted his nose in the air. "Oh, yes. I forgot about that, didn't I? No, I suppose you won't get the chance. But maybe you'll go to a family who plans to move. Or at least has boxes delivered. They really are fun."

Wayward realized that if Squeakers thought they were fun, they must be really, really fun, even though they only looked like boxes.

The phone rang and Miss Lady growled and stomped past Wayward and Squeakers, into the hallway and toward the kitchen. They followed.

"Oh, dear," Miss Lady said into the phone. "I'll be right over."

Without so much as a nod, Miss Lady left the house.

"What was that all about?" Wayward asked.

"I'm sure I have no idea."

"But she didn't even say good-bye. She always says good-bye."

Wayward Cat was sure that Squeakers looked worried, but the old cat merely shrugged and wandered off, onto the porch. Wayward dared not follow this time. He couldn't get lost outside right now because Miss Lady wasn't home to find him again. So he made his way back down the hallway and into the room full of boxes. Just being in the room, remembering the womp noises, sent shivers and chills along his back, making his hair stand up uncomfortably. This, he sensed, was a dangerous place. But Squeakers seemed to think boxes were for playing in. And if Miss Lady was going to send him away soon, maybe he could have an amazing adventure there right now.

Chapter Fourteen

The Daring Rescue

Many of Miss Lady's boxes were open and sitting atop short stacks in the middle of the room. But one very tall mountain of boxes towered in the back corner. She had a lot of unpacking to do, Wayward Cat thought.

"I will explore the land of boxes and find Miss Lady's lost treasure," he said. "She'll tell me what a helpful cat I am and she'll be so happy,

I'm sure she will let me stay."

He jumped onto low ledges and up onto higher peaks, clutching at the cardboard with his sharp claws, pulling himself up, and onto the boxes.

What does a pencil sharpener look like, he wondered. He dove into one box and felt the stack under him shake a bit. Under wads of newsprint, he found books and boxes of cards and unopened packages of pens and pencils. He wondered what they were all for and wished Miss Lady would unpack them and use them so he would know.

Nothing inside looked like it would sharpen pencils, so he hopped out and struggled to hold on to the side of the box, before dropping down into another on a lower stack. More paper, more books and rulers and cards. He hopped out and onto the floor and found more wadded up paper. He batted it around the room among the stacks, until he remembered he was on a great quest to find Miss Lady's treasure.

He climbed again, this time onto the tall stack in the corner. He struggled to pull himself all the way to the top, nearly to the ceiling. The mountain beneath him wobbled a bit, this way and that. His heart pounded and he started to shake.

"Oh, dear, this is just like the great curtain incident," he said. "Maybe I'm not so adventurous after all." He took in a deep breath and exhaled. "Miss Lady's lost treasure is not up high," he decided. "I must look for it down low, in a cave, perhaps."

He climbed down a bit and found an opening between boxes and hopped into it, but he misjudged the distance and fell out the other side with a plop. He was in a dark corner, up against the wall, boxes all around.

"Yes," he said. "The treasure is hidden here in the dark recesses of the earth."

He pounced on a scrap of paper. A treasure map! He chewed on it and spit it out. He saw a bug in the corner, buried in a bit of dust and cobwebs. He attacked, grabbed it and chewed on it. Then he spit that out, too.

"Yuck," he said. "That was old and dry."

He clawed at the cardboard boxes and chewed on the bits that he managed to shred. Then he spun in tiny circles and jumped into the air.

"There is no treasure here," he had to admit.

He looked up, searching for a place to jump

out. He saw the box he'd fallen from, but he could never get back up to it. He saw another low ledge and leapt for it, but fell back to the floor. He jumped again and tried to get hold of the side of the box with his claws, but he found nothing to hang on to. The box was too high. He was trapped at the bottom of a dark hole!

"Squeakers," he called. "Help."

He meowed and howled and called for help until his little voice was dry and hoarse. Finally, he heard the big cat.

"What is it this time?"

"I've fallen into a hole. Help me!"

He heard the cat jumping onto boxes one by one until he appeared overhead.

"There you are," the big cat said. "You're in an empty closet. Too bad Miss Lady didn't fill it with boxes. Then you wouldn't have fallen in."

"What do I do? I'm trapped."

"Jump."

"It's too high."

"Nonsense," he said. "Watch." Squeakers dropped into the hole beside him, with a bit of a bark upon landing. "It is tight in here." Then he leapt back onto the boxes. "See? Easy."

"But I'm too small. I can't jump that high.

I've tried."

"Don't be silly. Let me see you."

Wayward Cat tried to jump up to where Squeakers was and fell down again and again.

"You see? I'm too small."

The old cat sighed. "Well, Miss Lady should be home soon. She'll move the boxes and get you out."

"But I don't want to stay down here any longer. It's dark and cramped. I'm scared."

"Well, you haven't any choice."

With that, the old cat disappeared and left Wayward to meow and meow for the longest time. Eventually, the light at the top of the boxes dulled and Wayward's stomach growled. He heard Squeakers jumping up on the boxes again and saw his face looking down the hole at him.

"Where's Miss Lady?" Wayward Cat asked.

"I don't know. I'm getting worried. It's time for me to be fed."

"Has she ever left and not come back in time?"

"Yes. But she left extra food in the bowl."

"What if something terrible has happened?"

"Now, now. Let's not get ahead of ourselves. Perhaps she just forgot to leave extra food. We'll survive."

"But I'm stuck in a hole," Wayward Cat whined. "And I'm hungry."

Squeakers stared down at him and shook his head. "Oh, all right."

The big cat jumped down into the hole and said, "Stay still." He bit down firmly on the scruff of Wayward's neck, lifting him up, and Wayward's legs went limp as he dangled from the cat's big mouth. Suddenly, Squeakers bent low and leapt into the air landing on a box at the top of the stack. Then he hopped down the other boxes to the floor before setting Wayward Cat on the carpet.

Wayward shook and stumbled a bit. "Thank you," he said and rubbed against Squeakers' legs. "Oh, thank you so much."

"Humph."

"I thought you said boxes were fun."

"You play *in* them," Squeakers said. "Not *on* them."

"Oh." He'd have to remember that, if he ever decided to go near a box again.

"Let's go see if there's any food in the bowls," Squeakers said.

"What if there isn't any?"

"We'll just have to chew a hole through the bag."

"That sounds like something cats shouldn't do."

"This is an emergency," Squeakers said. "And anyway, if Miss Lady ever does come back, I'll tell her you did it."

Chapter Fifteen

A Very Bad Cat

Wayward Cat watched as Squeakers jumped up onto a shelf in the bathroom closet and started chewing on the bottom corner of the food bag.

"Are you sure this is a good idea?" He asked the big cat.

"We'll starve to death, otherwise."

"I am hungry. But I'm always hungry before feeding time. Maybe we should wait and see if Miss Lady comes home to feed us."

"Suit yourself. I'm not taking any chances. Miss Lady has disappeared. She didn't even take the big wheels out of the garage. She's gone, I tell you. Left us here to starve to death."

The more Squeakers chewed on the bag, the more anxious he became. At one point, a loud gurgle erupted from the big cat's stomach.

"You see?" He said and went back to ripping at the bag with his sharp teeth. "I'm going to starve! I'm going to starve! I must get this bag opened."

Suddenly a loud rip was followed by a rain of kibble onto Wayward's head.

Squeakers had managed to make a large hole in the bottom of the bag, and kibble poured out onto the shelf and to the floor below.

When Miss Lady arrived home a short time later, she was not happy. As soon as the front door of the house opened, Squeakers dropped down from the shelf where he was gobbling up kibble and ran out into the kitchen to hide, leaving Wayward behind.

"Squeakers!" Miss Lady shouted as soon as she saw the mess. "You are a very bad cat."

She stomped out of the bathroom and disappeared.

"But I'm still hungry," Wayward Cat meowed.

He sat and patiently waited. Miss Lady had never forgotten to feed him before. Perhaps she only needed to scold Squeakers and then she would come and pour the kibble. When she returned, she had a roll of tape and she carefully taped up the hole Squeakers had made. Then she put kibble into both bowls.

Squeakers came running into the bathroom.

"It wasn't me," he was saying. "It was the other one."

"You behaved badly," Miss Lady told him. She waved a finger at him while he ate.

"How did she know it was me? Did you tell her?"

"I'm too small to get up onto that shelf," Wayward Cat told him. "She knew it had to be you."

"Humph," the big cat said and went back to eating.

The next morning, Miss Lady called to Wayward Cat and picked him up and took him outside. As she carried him away from the house, he panicked.

He called out to Squeakers, "She's taking me away!"

But Squeakers was not sitting on a window sill and probably didn't hear him.

"Good-bye, Squeakers," he cried. And he wondered if Miss Lady did think he was the one who chewed open the kibble bag. What if he'd left claw holes in the curtains? Or perhaps he'd made a mess with the boxes. Maybe she'd decided she didn't want a bad cat.

Chapter Sixteen

Wayward Cat Comforts Jane

Miss Lady carried Wayward Cat down the road just a bit and up to another house. She knocked at the door and an older lady opened it. Their cheerful chatting reminded him of birds and the other woman reached out to pet him, but Wayward was too sad to enjoy it. This new house smelled like moth balls and cleaning fluids. And dirty laundry.

He was carried through the house and down a hall, and the old woman was saying, "Thank you," over and over again. "I can't thank you enough for taking us to the hospital yesterday," she said.

Wayward Cat wondered if the hospital was the same as the vet. He found himself in a room painted pink and Miss Lady put him down on a soft bed where a little girl was sitting up against pillows. She set her book down on her lap and smiled at Wayward. She seemed nice enough, he thought, with pale hair and eyes and freckles across her nose.

"There you are," Miss Lady said. "A kitten, just for you."

Wayward tried to purr, but he was too sad. It wasn't that he didn't like the color pink, or little girls. After Mama Cat had told him about people kittens, he'd wanted to meet one someday. He just thought he'd get to stay with Miss Lady forever. And he already missed Squeakers very much.

The little girl reached out and pet him and he offered her a weak meow. Then he noticed one of her arms wrapped up in white plaster; it was stiff and only her hand was exposed.

"She's injured. I suppose she needs me," he thought. And with that, he stepped forward and climbed onto the book in her lap. He let her nuzzle him and finally, he purred.

"Wayward Cat," Miss Lady said. "This is Jane."

"We'll see how it goes," the old lady said.

Wayward watched as Miss Lady left the room

and he waited until he heard the front door open and close. He got off the young girl's book, so she could read, and curled himself up by her side. He was too frightened yet to explore. He tried to think of Mama Cat. What would Mama Cat say? And he remembered.

"You will miss me," Mama had told him. "But you will grow to love your new home soon enough. Just give it time."

Wayward whimpered and put his face between his paws. Jane pet him and he felt better. Then he heard a bark. He jumped up and trembled. The smell of dirty laundry seemed suddenly strong around him.

"That's just Barney," Jane said. "He lives in the back yard. He only comes inside once in a while."

Wayward looked around the room for dogs. He was sure he didn't like them. No matter what Mama Cat said, he didn't think he could ever grow to love one. When he was sure the dog was not in the room with him, he climbed down off the bed and began to sniff about and see what he could make of his new home.

Six pairs of shoes were lined up neatly on the floor in a closet. Below the only window, sat a clean desk and a chest of drawers. A bookshelf holding a few books and some statues of cats and fairies sat next to the bed. He chewed at a fairy wing on the bottom shelf and Jane giggled.

"Oh, dear," Wayward Cat said. "It will take all of my imagination to manage adventures here. It's much too organized." But it would have to do.

He imagined Squeakers back at Miss Lady's house, the house he once thought of as home. The big cat would be in the outside room stalking the squirrel, or curled up on his bed by the window snoozing. He'd have all the food to himself now. And he wouldn't have to rescue Wayward from his adventures. He wondered if Squeakers would miss him at all. Probably not, he thought.

He sniffed some more, learning all the new smells, and then made his way under the bed. No dust bunnies to keep him company. No dead bugs in the corner. Wayward clawed his way back up onto the bed to sit next to Jane. He was going to have to become a dull cat.

Chapter Seventeen

A Very Dull Adventure

After a while, Jane scooted down under the covers of her bed, winced as if in pain, and fell asleep. Wayward Cat decided it was a good time to try to find an adventure. He hopped off the bed and looked around the room. The most likely place for adventure would be up on the desk. There was a window he could look out of. Maybe he would see Miss Lady's house. Maybe Squeakers would be sitting on a window sill looking for him.

The chair was high, but he managed to jump onto it and then up onto the desk. He went to the window and looked out. There were no houses to be seen. This must be the back yard, he thought. There was a row of big shrubby plants along a wooden fence with a dirt path in front of them. And there was Barney, a large round dog, his tongue hanging out, walking along the path. He walked to the left and disappeared. After a moment, he reappeared at the window. Wayward jumped and hissed. But the dog kept walking and vanished again briefly, only to show up at the hedges.

"Why, he's just walking in circles. What a silly dog."

Wayward Cat waited at the window and each time the big dog passed he pawed at the glass and hissed. After six visits to the window, Barney finally noticed him. He put his paws up on the outer sill and barked. Wayward skittered backward until he fell onto the chair. He pounced to the floor and ran under the bed. Barney barked again and again until he finally went away, back to his walking circle.

"Well, that was an adventure of sorts."

Wayward Cat decided there was treasure in Jane's shoes in the closet and he set about digging it out of them. He sat atop each shoe, reached his paws into the toe and scratched and scratched. He gnawed on bows and jewels stuck to the tops. He leapt and pounced and wrestled the shoes until he was tired.

"I suppose I could do that once a day," he

said. "But what else?"

He found he was able to jump onto the second shelf of the bookcase. There were three books there and he attacked them and tried to chew the corners. Then he decided to push a fairy statue to the floor. He pawed at it and pawed at it, and moved it closer and closer to the edge, until it fell to the carpet with a thud.

Wayward Cat sat on the shelf and looked down at it.

"Hm," he said. "I suppose I could do that once a day, too. And then, when I get bigger, I can get up on the higher shelves and knock things off them."

And he supposed Jane might sometimes leave a drawer open in the chest and he could rummage in there and see what he could find. The room didn't have string, or fabric mice, but it would have to do.

Barney barked again and Wayward Cat looked up to see him jumping up and down at the window. His big head rose and then vanished. It rose again, his tongue flapping about, and disappeared again.

"Maybe I could get used to him," Wayward said. But he trembled at the thought.

When Jane stirred and sat back up, Wayward Cat climbed the covers onto the bed and curled up at her feet. It would just have to do, he told himself. The smells were wrong, of course. Too clean and disinfected. There weren't any toys. There was a dog. There were no places to hide. Oh, Squeakers, he thought. *I miss you. I want to go back to Miss Lady's house.*

Chapter Eighteen

Home Again

When the light outside began to dim, Wayward Cat heard Jane's front door open and close. He thought he recognized a voice, but was afraid to hope.

"We have a visitor," the old woman said as she opened the door to his new room.

Wayward jumped up and meowed when Miss Lady walked in. He was so happy to see her, he twirled in a few circles and pounced on the bedspread.

"I'm so glad you came to visit me," he meowed.

Miss Lady picked him up and pet him.

"How did it go?" She said.

"It was awful," he tried to tell her. "There are no things to play with and there is a dog outside."

"Well?" The older woman said to Jane.

"I feel fine," the little girl said. "I haven't sneezed once and my eyes aren't puffy at all."

"Are you sure?"

"Mom, I'm sure. Oh, please, please."

"Oh, all right."

Jane cheered and said thank you again and again. But Wayward Cat was just glad to have Miss Lady holding him, even if it was only for a little while. To his surprise, Miss Lady carried him out of Jane's room, while talking to the old woman.

Maybe she will forget to put me down, he thought. Maybe she will carry me all the way to her house and be too tired to bring me back. When Miss Lady went to the front door and said good-bye to the old woman and carried him outside and across the street, Wayward Cat was confused.

"You did a very good job comforting Jane," Miss Lady said. "And you helped show her mom that she didn't have a cat allergy. Can you imagine someone being allergic to cats?"

Wayward wasn't sure what Miss Lady was saying, but it was certain she hadn't just forgotten to leave him with Jane. She carried him into her house, set him down in the kitchen, and said,

"Here you are, back home where you belong."

Home. That was a word he knew. Wayward Cat couldn't help himself. He scrambled across the floor and into the living room, calling for Squeakers.

"Where are you? Squeakers! Squeakers! Where are you?"

Around the house he ran. All the smells were just right. The foods. The dust. The outside when the windows were open. There were the pieces of string, attached to plastic poles stuck to the wall. There was his puffy chair and the book cases where he could hide. His fabric mice. There was the clean room with the glass table. And there was his room and his bed and his front window. He finally found the old cat in the bathroom sitting by the food bowls.

"Squeakers!" Wayward Cat stopped and panted, trying to catch his breath. "I'm back."

"So you are."

"I'm home. Miss Lady said I'm home."

"So I see."

"I get to stay! I live here now. With you."

"Humph."

"Is that okay? Squeakers, can I stay? I have all sorts of ideas for new adventures."

The old cat sighed, walked over and plopped himself down on top of Wayward Cat making him squeak.

"Squeakers," Miss Lady called. "Stop that."

But Wayward Cat laughed. "Do it again. Do it again."

Squeak!

Also by Dana Trantham

Children of Path: The Kell Stone Prophecy Book One
The Wretched: The Kell Stone Prophecy Book Two

Coming Soon

The Story Runner

Watch for more books in the Wayward Cat series
from
Wayward Cat Publishing
www.waywardcatpublishing.com

Made in the USA
Columbia, SC
14 September 2018